LITTLENOSE

Littlenose had a green pebble to spend, so he was very excited when Father took him to market. What he really wanted was a mammoth, but even in a mammoth sale they cost too much. Then he came across a reject – the smallest, woolliest and saddest mammoth imaginable . . .

Littlenose knew that Mother wouldn't allow animals – even pet mice – into the cave. But when Littlenose got lost in the dark and his new mammoth helped him to find the way home, she agreed it could stay.

Littlenose called his mammoth Two-Eyes, and together they had lots of adventures.

Littlenose was invented for John Grant's own children, but was soon entertaining millions more when he first appeared on Jackanory in 1968.

The Neanderthal boy whose pet was bought in a mammoth sale, whose mother is in despair at the rough treatment he gives his furs, and whose exasperated father sometimes threatens to feed him to a sabre-toothed tiger, is everybody's favourite.

Besides gaining wide acceptance in Great Britain, the Littlenose stories have been translated into German, French, Italian, Dutch, Spanish and Japanese.

LITTLENOSE

John Grant

Illustrated by the author

BBC/KNIGHT

Copyright © John Grant 1968
First published 1968 by the British Broadcasting Corporation

This edition published 1983 by the British Broadcasting
Corporation/Knight Books

Third impression 1984

British Library C.I.P.

Grant, John, *1930–*
   Littlenose.
   I. Title
   823′.914[J]   PZ7

   ISBN 0 340 33117 8
     (0 563 20173 8 BBC)

Printed and bound in Great Britain for the British
Broadcasting Corporation, 35 Marylebone High Street,
London W1M 4AA and Hodder and Stoughton
Paperbacks, a division of Hodder and Stoughton Ltd.,
Mill Road, Dunton Green, Sevenoaks, Kent (Editorial
Office: 47 Bedford Square, London, WC1 3DP) by
Richard Clay (The Chaucer Press) Ltd,
Bungay, Suffolk

Littlenose Meets Two-Eyes

Littlenose was a boy who lived long, long ago. His people were called the Neanderthal Folk. In the days when they lived, the world was very cold. It was called the Ice Age.

There were lots of wild animals. Lions, tigers, bears and wolves had thick furry coats to keep them warm. Even the rhinoceros, and a kind of elephant called a mammoth, were big woolly creatures.

The Neanderthal Folk were stocky, sturdy people with short necks and big noses. They were very proud of their noses, which were large and snuffly. Littlenose got his name because his nose was no bigger than a berry.

Littlenose's home was not a house, but a cave where he lived with his Father and

Mother. Near the front of the cave a huge fire
was always burning. This kept the family
warm, and also frightened away wild
creatures, which was just as well because
there was no door on the cave.

Sometimes Littlenose was naughty, and that
could be dangerous. A child who
strayed from his family cave, or loitered on an
errand, might be eaten by a sabre-tooth tiger,
or squashed flat as a pancake by a woolly
rhinoceros.

6

But today Littlenose had been very naughty indeed. While his parents were hunting, he had let the fire go out.

Now he sat at the back of the cave and watched Father trying to re-light it. Father had two stones called flints which he banged together to make a spark. (There were no matches in those days.) But he couldn't strike a spark.

"Perhaps you need a new flint," said Mother.

"I'll need a new son if he lets the fire out again," grumbled Father. Littlenose expected to be thrown to the bears right away.

However, as they had no fire, Father blocked the cave entrance with rocks to keep out wild beasts. In the morning they had a cold breakfast. Father got ready to go for the flint.

"Have you enough money?" said Mother.

"I think so," said Father, and pulled out a handful of the coloured pebbles which they used for money.

He kissed Mother goodbye, and was just going when Littlenose said, "Can I come too?"

For a moment Father said nothing. Then: "After the way you behaved, yesterday?" he exclaimed. "Oh, all right," and off he went, leaving Littlenose to follow.

"Goodbye, Littlenose," Mother called after him. "Be good. And always look both ways before you cross."

But Littlenose wasn't listening. He was thinking about his secret. He had a pebble of his own. A green pebble, which he had found by the river. He had never been to a market before. But he was sure he would see something worth buying today.

They made their way by a woodland path. Father strode along with his club in his hand,

and Littlenose skipped gaily behind him.
Ahead, the path was crossed by a broad
animal trail. Littlenose was about to dash
straight across, when a cuff on the ear nearly
knocked him down.

"Don't you *ever* do what Mother tells you?"
said Father, angrily. Shamefaced, Littlenose
stood on the grass verge and:

> Looked right!
> Looked left!
> And right again!

As he looked right the second time, a herd of
woolly rhinoceros came round a bend. He and
Father dived into the bushes. They lay hidden
as the great beasts lumbered by. Their small
eyes blinked through their fur, and their long
horns looked very dangerous.

When the rhinos had passed, Littlenose and Father went on their way.

Littlenose felt he had been walking for ever. But soon they left the woods and began climbing a grassy hillside. At last they came to a circle of trees. Littlenose realised that this was the market.

There seemed to be hundreds of people. Littlenose hadn't thought there were so many people in the whole world. He trotted behind Father, and he was bumped, pushed, trodden on, tripped over and shouted at. The sheer noise made him speechless – but not for long.

Suddenly: "I'm hungry," he said.

"You're always hungry," grumbled Father. But he bought each of them a steaming hot hunk of meat from a man who was roasting a deer over a fire.

Then he went over to an old man who was sitting under a tree. There was a sign with his name on it.

At least, Littlenose thought it was his name.

When he got closer, he saw that it had once read:

But the words were faded with the weather. Only "Skin" and "Flint" could be made out now. Most people thought it was the old man's name.

Neither Father nor the old man seemed in a hurry to settle about the new flint. Littlenose soon grew bored.

He wandered through the market, looking here and listening there. Everyone was bustling about buying the things they couldn't find or make for themselves. There were bone and ivory combs, and needles and pins. There were strange nuts, fruits and berries. And there were furs. Hundreds and hundreds of furs. From tiny mink and ermine to enormous white bear skins from the far north.

But Littlenose didn't see anything he wanted to buy. He had almost decided to keep his pebble for another day, when, over the heads of the crowd, he saw a sign.

MAMMOTH SALE
GENUINE REDUCTIONS

Littlenose pushed forward. In a clear space, a little man stood on a tree stump.

"Five red pebbles I'm bid," he shouted. "Five! Going at five! Going! Going! GONE! Sold to the gentleman in the lion-skin for five red pebbles."

The gentleman in the lion-skin counted out his money. Then a huge woolly mammoth was led over to him.

"Oh," thought Littlenose, "if only I could buy one of those. I would march home, leading him by his trunk. Everyone would

cheer. When I got home I would . . . oh, dear no. I forgot. I'm not even allowed pet mice in the cave. Anyway, a mammoth would hardly get its tail through the door. And that's about all I could buy with my pebble."

And, feeling very sad, Littlenose walked away. He sat down by the mammoth pen to rest. The pen was built of huge logs and was too high to see over.

Suddenly he jumped. Something soft and warm had tickled his neck.

It was a trunk – a very little one.

Littlenose looked through the bars of the pen. He saw the smallest, woolliest, saddest mammoth you could imagine. He climbed up and reached over the top rail to stroke its furry ears.

Suddenly he was seized by the scruff of his neck. A voice said: "And what are you doing, young man?"

It was the man who owned the mammoths.

"Please," said Littlenose, "I was just looking at the mammoth."

"Don't tell stories," said the man. "We've sold them all."

But at that moment the trunk came through the bars again. It tickled the man's leg and he dropped Littlenose.

"They've done it again," the man shouted to his assistant, who came running. "Slipped in a reject! It's much too small to sell. And look, the eyes don't match! One's red and one's green. Who's going to buy this sort of animal?"

"I will," said Littlenose, holding out his pebble.

Looking very relieved the man said: "Well, I can't charge you more than eight white pebbles for a reject." He took the green pebble from Littlenose, and gave him two white ones as change. The assistant opened the pen, and the little mammoth trotted out.

"One red eye and one green eye," said Littlenose. "That makes two eyes. I shall call you that. Come along, Two-Eyes."

Littlenose stopped and bought a bundle of bone needles for Mother with his last two pebbles. The market was almost deserted now.

He started looking for Father, but Father found him first.

"Where *have* you been?" he shouted.

"Do you like my mammoth?" asked Littlenose.

"Mammoth? MAMMOTH?" roared Father. "Are you playing with other people's property? Take it back where you found it.

16

No, wait, we haven't time." He waved his arms in the air, and gave a loud yell. Two-Eyes went scampering away into the trees.

"But he's mine. I *bought* him," wailed Littlenose.

But Father wasn't listening – he was already striding away down the hillside. Littlenose hurried after him. The evening mist began to close in, and the sun became a dull red ball low in the sky.

"Don't dawdle, you'll get lost," called out Father. But Littlenose kept tripping in the long grass. Each time he looked up, it was darker, and even harder to see his Father.

He ran on, stumbling and tripping.

Then he fell!

When he got up again, he was alone. "Father!" he called. "FATHER!" But all he heard was the echo of his own voice.

He began to run. He had never been lost before, and he was very frightened. All sorts of terrible things might be waiting in the mist to

17

jump out at him. As he ran, the sun set. It became pitch dark.

All around him he could hear animals growling and snorting. They rustled in the undergrowth, and brushed past him as he ran. He stopped to catch his breath. There was a sound behind him. It was growing louder.

Littlenose began to run again. But, as fast as he ran, the noise came closer. Suddenly he tripped again and fell.

Too frightened to move, Littlenose lay with his eyes closed. The sound grew louder. He could hear an animal breathing, but he dared not look up.

At the cave, Mother looked out as darkness fell. There was a sound of footsteps, and Father groped his way in.

"Where's Littlenose?" asked Mother.

"Isn't he here?" said Father. "I thought the young rascal must have hurried home ahead of me."

Oh," said Mother, "he must be lost out there in the dark. You must find him!"

Quickly, Father lit the fire, took a branch for a torch, and turned back the way he had come.

The mist had gone and the moon was shining. The path lay clear before him. There were animal sounds among the trees. But there was no sign of Littlenose.

Then something moved towards him. Father's torch glinted on a pair of eyes. One red eye. One green eye. It was a small mammoth, and sitting on its back was Littlenose.

"Hello, Father," he said. "I got lost, and Two-Eyes followed me and brought me home."

Mother saw the strange procession approaching the cave. Father was leading Two-Eyes by the trunk. Littlenose, his head nodding, sat on the mammoth's back.

A few moments later, Mother was tucking Littlenose in bed. He held out a little bundle. "I bought you some needles at the market," he said, and fell asleep.

The little mammoth was patiently waiting outside. Father took its trunk gently in his hand. He led it past the fire and into the corner where Littlenose slept. With a contented sigh and looking for all the world like an enormous ball of wool, Two-Eyes fell asleep as well.

The Shell Necklace

Littlenose's aunt had a shell necklace. She was wearing it when she visited Mother one day, and it was really beautiful. Mother was rather envious, and Littlenose thought it was a dreadful shame that she didn't have one.

After the visitor had left, Littlenose said, "Mother, that was a very nice necklace Auntie was wearing. What is it made of?" He had never seen shells before.

"Shells," said Mother, "sea shells. Now off you go to bed."

Littlenose lay in bed and thought and thought. Somehow, he decided, his Mother would have a shell necklace, and it would be bigger and more beautiful than his aunt's – or anyone else's. But he wasn't awfully sure what sea shells were, or where he would get them. Father, he decided, was the person most likely to know. He would ask him in the morning.

After breakfast, next morning, Father settled down to work on some flints that needed chipping. These were the ordinary flints used for the heads of axes and spears, not the special fire-making ones. In a moment or two, Littlenose came up to him and said: "Father, where do sea shells come from?"

Father looked up. "From the sea," he replied, and carried on chipping.

"Where's the sea?" asked Littlenose.

"That's where the river goes," snapped Father, and started banging his flints so loudly that any other questions were useless.

Littlenose wandered off to where Two-Eyes was grazing by the river bank. "Tomorrow," he said, "we are going to the sea. We must leave early, before anyone is awake. We shall follow the river until we get there. We are going to get Mother the best necklace in the world."

Littlenose slept very little that night. He kept watching the door of the cave, where the starry sky was visible beyond the fire. At long last, as the first paleness appeared in the east, he woke Two-Eyes, and together they tip-toed out into the morning mist, and set out for the sea.

They were barely out of sight of home when they surprised a large bear in the river. The sight of breakfast in the shape of a tender boy and a plump mammoth so astounded the bear that it just stood up, open-mouthed, dribbling with pleasure. Littlenose and Two-Eyes, however, ran on as fast as they could.

When the bear suddenly realised that its breakfast was trying to escape, it gave a howl of fury and charged after them. It might have caught them too, but it missed its footing on a mossy rock, and plunged head first into a deep pool. When Littlenose looked back from a safe distance, the bear had climbed back onto the bank, and was jumping up and down with

rage, in a great shower of spray from its bedraggled fur.

A mile or two further on they heard such a loud roaring that they almost turned back. Expecting to meet some hideous monster, they were surprised to find that it was the river itself. It leaped high over a cliff in a beautiful waterfall, and it was the water thundering on the rocks and echoing between the banks, which had frightened them.

It was much further than Littlenose had imagined. He had somehow pictured himself

reaching the sea, finding sea shells, and being home for lunch. But, by late afternoon they were trudging wearily over a wide, sandy heath, with the river flowing, broad and majestic, beside them.

They were both very tired by now, and Littlenose was plodding on with his head down when he nearly stumbled over a large woolly rhinoceros which was enjoying a quiet snooze. They were very frightened. But the rhinoceros just lumbered to its feet, peered through its fur at them with sleepy, short-sighted eyes; then, to their great relief, went muttering and grumbling away into the bushes with an occasional backward, irritable glance.

Soon it was almost evening. The sky was red, and they were very, very tired. Littlenose took a few more weary steps and . . . there was the sea!

It was enormous! Littlenose had never imagined anything so big. It stretched far away, far into the mist. The river flowed out between some low sand-hills and joined the sea.

"Now for the sea shells," said Littlenose, and he and Two-Eyes ran down the long grassy bank, over the sand dunes and on to the beach.

The beach was very narrow, and they soon reached the water's edge. Small waves lapped quietly on the soft sand, and Littlenose peered into them. But there were no shells. He waded in a little way, but still there were none. With Two-Eyes, he hurried up and down the beach, but all he could find was dried sea-weed and smooth pieces of driftwood. Littlenose was almost crying with disappointment. But it was growing dark, and he thought to himself,

"Maybe I'll be able to find shells better in daylight. I think we'll wait till morning."

Leading Two-Eyes, he climbed back up to the edge of the heath, and after eating some fruit from a large bramble bush for his supper, he settled down in a sheltered hollow to sleep.

The sun was just rising when Littlenose awoke. "Come on, Two-Eyes," he shouted. "We must find those sea shells." He dashed forward and stopped in amazement.

The sea had gone!

The beach now stretched away into the morning mist. The sand was wet, and there were pools of water, otherwise you would never have known that the sea had been there at all. He ran across the wet, rippled sand.

"Come on, Two-Eyes," he called. "We must find the sea, or we won't find any shells."

They splashed on for a little further, then Littlenose spotted something small and white at his feet. He picked it up.

It was a sea shell! He found another, then

another, and another!

Soon he was picking up shells as fast as he could. White ones, pink ones, blue ones and yellow ones. Some were flat like small plates, some were long and pointed like a horn, while some looked just like snail shells. In a few moments, Littlenose had as many as he could stuff inside his furs. Then he danced with joy, up and down, round and round, leaving his footprints on the wet sand. The patterns of the footprints so pleased him that he made some more. Then he knelt down and made hand prints on the sand. This was fun! He drew a circle with his finger, then made two eyes, a nose, and a wide grinning mouth. It was a man! Littlenose laughed with pleasure.

He drew another man. Then a mammoth.
Then a bear. He wondered what to draw next.
Before he could draw anything, there was a
snort of alarm from Two-Eyes. He had been
standing dozing some distance away, when a
splash of cold water aroused him. Waves were
lapping round his feet.

The sea had come back!

While Littlenose had been playing on the
sand, the water had quietly crept up and
around him, and now he and Two-Eyes were
on a little island. Even as he watched, the
island grew smaller.

"Run, Two-Eyes, run!" shouted Littlenose.

They ran together, splashing through small waves. The water barely came over their ankles, and they were soon almost half-way to safety. But then it began to grow deeper. Soon it was up to Littlenose's knees, then his waist, and he could walk only very slowly.

"You'll have to carry me, Two-Eyes," he said, and climbed on to the mammoth's back.

Two-Eyes trudged on, his feet sinking in the soft sand. The water soon reached Littlenose's waist again. It rose and rose until Two-Eyes had to raise his trunk in the air to breathe. All that could be seen was Littlenose's head, and the tip of Two-Eyes' trunk above the water.

But now they were past the worst. The water became shallower, and soon Two-Eyes was plodding through the last of the small waves and up the beach. Littlenose slid from his back, and the two of them stood while the water drained off them. Then they went back to the bramble bush and had a late breakfast. Before setting off for home, Littlenose made certain that the shells were still safe inside his furs.

There were no adventures on the way back. They were just passing the pool where they had met the bear, when they saw a group of people coming towards them.

One of them was Father. "Hi!" he shouted. Littlenose ran towards him. "Thank goodness you're safe," said Father, "we were all very worried. Where have you been?"

"I went to the sea," said Littlenose, "to get shells for Mother's necklace."

Father didn't say anything, and Littlenose knew he was very, very angry. Taking

Littlenose by the ear, he marched him up the valley and home. Littlenose wondered what was going to happen to him.

Actually nothing did. Mother was so relieved to see him again that she cried. And when Father had strung the shells together, there were plenty to make a necklace for Mother, and enough left over to make her a beautiful bracelet for each wrist.

The Great Elk

The cave where Littlenose lived with his
Mother and Father and Two-Eyes was beside a
river which flowed down into a broad valley.
It wasn't a very big river. It was shallow
enough to wade right across in most places,
and only in the spring, when melting snow and
ice made it into a great torrent, was it really
dangerous.

The river became narrower and narrower
towards the higher reaches of the valley. At the
very head of the valley was a steep rocky cliff,
and the river tumbled down in small waterfalls
from the little lake where it began. Littlenose
loved to walk right through the valley, then
scramble up the crooked path zig-zagging up
the cliff-face to reach the lake.

34

One day in late summer, Littlenose and Two-Eyes were lying in the grass by the lake, watching the fish dart about in the green depths. Two-Eyes was still trying to catch his breath after the climb from the valley, which was a bit steep for a rather plump young mammoth. Littlenose, however, just couldn't stay still.

He skimmed stones across the waters of the lake. He pulled the fluffy heads off the cotton grass and stuck them all over Two-Eyes' black fur. Then he began to make loud, shrill noises by blowing on a broad blade of grass. He did this right in Two-Eyes' ear, and Two-Eyes grumpily got up and stalked over to a large bush, out of Littlenose's way, where he settled down in the shade.

Two-Eyes had hardly sat down when he jumped up again with a loud snort. Littlenose came running to see what was the matter.

Two-Eyes had pricked himself on a sharp bony object sticking out from beneath the bush.

Littlenose bent down and tried to pick it up. But he found to his surprise that it was part of something much bigger. He pulled with all his might and, in a few moments, he was looking at something very strange. It was bleached by the weather, and was broken in one place, but it was obviously an antler. And, what an antler!

Littlenose had seen the antlers of the deer killed and brought home by his father, but this was enormous. It was bigger than Littlenose himself. He tried to lift it, but it was far too heavy, he couldn't even drag it along the ground.

It was almost evening by now, so Littlenose sadly left his find and set off for home with Two-Eyes. That night at supper, he said: "I found an old antler today, up on the moor. It was a giant antler. Bigger than I. I couldn't even lift it."

Now usually when Littlenose told his parents about all the wonderful things he had seen and done, they would tell him to stop talking nonsense and making up stories. This time, however, Father looked at him open-mouthed, then said: "A giant antler? Are you quite sure, Littlenose? You're not making it up, are you?"

Littlenose wondered if perhaps he had done something wrong. "It was a very big antler," he said. "Two-Eyes pricked himself on it."

Father's voice was hushed. "The Great Elk," he said. "Some have heard his roaring. A few have seen his tracks. Fewer still have actually found an antler. And no one has ever seen him!"

"What is he?" asked Littlenose impatiently.

"He is the King of the wild beasts," said Father. "He stands as tall as a mammoth, and his mighty antlers blot out the sun itself as he passes. When he roars, the leaves tremble. When he stamps, the ground shakes beneath his great hooves."

"I wish I could see the Great Elk some day," said Littlenose.

"You've seen his antler, which is more than most people," said Father. "Now off to bed, we're going berry-picking early tomorrow."

Next morning, carrying baskets woven from reeds, the family set off for the moors where the bilberries grew in great patches of blue-black on the low bushes. It was almost mid-day when they arrived, and they had something to eat before starting to gather the fruit.

At first Littlenose thought the fruit-picking fun. He quickly filled his small basket and then emptied it into Mother's big one. He did this several times, but each time he took longer, until at last he put his basket down, and began to chase Two-Eyes, who had been peacefully dozing in the grass. But Two-Eyes was quite ready to play now. They ran round gorse bushes and over heather clumps. The berry-picking was quite forgotten.

They scampered to the top of a low hillock and there, on the other side, they saw what looked like a lovely place to play. The bright green ground was smooth and level, with a few pools of water – much better than the rough, tussocky heather! With shouts of glee,

Littlenose raced down the slope, and Two-Eyes
followed. Suddenly a shout from Father
stopped them in their tracks. He came striding
past them without a word, a large stone
clutched in his hand. Stopping on the edge of
the bright green ground, Father threw the
stone. Littlenose watched it fall with a *plop*!
To his astonishment, instead of lying there, it
sank slowly from sight, until only a dark patch
on the green showed where it had fallen.

"That," said Father, "is a bog; and if you were to set foot on the green moss you would be sucked down and drowned. There are many places like this on the moor, and you must keep clear of them. If you are ever lost in the mist or darkness, stay where you are. One wrong step and you would be gone for ever."

Littlenose listened in silence. The bright green moss did not look so attractive now. It seemed evil, and he was glad to hurry after Father to where Mother was still collecting berries.

Picking up his basket, Littlenose began gathering fruit again. He'd picked quite a few berries when he noticed some others which seemed much bigger than the ones he had. He emptied his basket, hurried to the new patch and started picking again. He had hardly begun picking this time, before he dashed off again to some more which looked sweeter . . . then bigger . . . then sweeter again. Until, at last, he realised that he was hot and weary, with only a few berries to show for all his effort. He looked around him. Two-Eyes was with him, but there was no sign of Mother or Father. He called out.

There was no answer. The only sound was the sighing of the wind. Even the bees, which had been buzzing and bumbling all day among the purple heather, had gone as evening approached.

Littlenose climbed on to a large boulder, and looked all around. In the fading light, the moor stretched on all sides. Several times he

thought he saw his parents, but when they didn't move, he realised it was only rocks or lonely birch trees. He tried to remember which way he had come, and set off in what he hoped was the right direction. Once he was sure he had found his own footprints, and a moment later he spotted a cluster of squashed bilberries. But already it was almost completely dark, and he blundered on, hoping at any moment to hear Father's voice calling him.

Two-Eyes was trotting along close behind him when suddenly he bumped right into Littlenose. "Back, Two-Eyes, back," cried Littlenose, stopping dead.

He had suddenly felt the ground quiver under his feet, and a cold clamminess gripped his ankles. He staggered back on to firm ground, and leaned against Two-Eyes' shaggy side until his heart stopped thumping. He knelt down, and carefully felt the ground. It was cold and damp, and as he pressed down, icy water oozed up between his fingers. It was a bog, and he shuddered at his narrow escape.

They started walking again, but a few moments later it was Two-Eyes who drew back and snorted. Another bog! Littlenose looked around. It was now so dark that it was impossible to tell the dangerous moss from solid ground. Littlenose remembered what his father had said, and decided they must stay where they were.

Two-Eyes, who usually took things very

calmly, had found a grassy hollow, and was already asleep. Littlenose snuggled against the mammoth's furry body, and settled down to wait for daylight.

He must have dozed, because suddenly he found himself sitting upright beside Two-Eyes in bright moonlight. Two-Eyes was also sitting up, his little trunk stretched out, sniffing, and his big hairy ears spread wide to catch the slightest sound. Whatever had disturbed them either had gone, or was keeping very quiet.

Suddenly, everything went dark. The moonlight was blotted out by a dark shape which cast a deep shadow over the hollow. Littlenose glanced fearfully upwards. Was it a rhinoceros? A giant bear? The shadow moved – and the moonlight glinted for a moment on a familiar shape. It was an antler. No, it was a pair of antlers, wide and sweeping, with sharp points catching the light. A flowing mane stirred in the night wind and, as his eyes

became accustomed to the dark, Littlenose
made out the majestic shape of a great animal
standing on the rim of the hollow.

"The Great Elk," breathed Littlenose. "The
King of the wild beasts."

46

The animal took a step towards them, then turned and walked away. A moment later he was back, and again took a step forward before disappearing, but this time making a low rumbling noise deep in his throat.

"What is he saying, Two-Eyes?" said Littlenose. "What is it? Does he want us to follow him?"

The little mammoth got to his feet and scrambled after the Great Elk. Littlenose followed them.

For hours they walked and stumbled after the huge creature. Sometimes they seemed to be walking in circles, but always on hard ground, clear of the treacherous bogs. Both Littlenose and Two-Eyes were almost asleep on their feet, when at last the Great Elk led them to a small pine wood. There he gave a last throaty grunt, and turned away into the darkness.

Almost immediately, Littlenose heard voices, and Father appeared, with Mother close behind him.

"We got lost," said Littlenose, as Mother picked him up. "But I remembered what Father said about the bogs, and we stayed where we were. Then the Great Elk brought us back to you."

Father looked sharply at Littlenose, and was about to say something, but Mother put her finger to her lips. Littlenose was asleep.

It was now daylight. Mother, with Littlenose in her arms, and Father with the berry basket, started to return home. As they moved off, Father paused and said: "Look!"

In the sandy soil, close by where they had found Littlenose, leading back into the wide expanse of the moor, were the tracks of gigantic cloven hoofs.

The Straightnoses

One day, Father and Littlenose set off up the valley on a fishing trip. Father carried his fishing spear and Littlenose was trying to walk with the basket on his head. Father did not usually like taking Littlenose, because Littlenose had his own ideas about fishing. He liked to dance and shout on the bank, hurling stones into the water, which frightened every fish for miles. But Mother had declared that a whole day with Littlenose was very tiring, and that it was time that Father took a turn at looking after him.

When they reached the lake, Father said: "Littlenose, why don't you play over there? Or why not look for dry sticks, and then we can make a fire, cook some fish and have a picnic before going home?"

Littlenose dashed away, and Father settled down to his fishing. He caught more fish than usual and soon the basket was bulging. Father laid down his spear and looked at the sun. It was high in the sky – almost mid-day.

"Littlenose," he called, "I'm ready for the firewood."

Littlenose came running. He was filthy. His face and hands were black as soot, but he dropped a big bundle of sticks at Father's feet.

"What on earth have you been doing?" asked Father.

"I couldn't help it," said Littlenose. "The sticks are all dirty."

"These sticks have been burnt," said Father. "Where did you find them?"

"Over there," said Littlenose, pointing. "There are lots more."

Father hurried over, took one quick look, and next moment was running with Littlenose back to the lake. He picked up his spear and the basket of fish, then took Littlenose by the hand again – and they started to run.

Over the moor they went. Down the cliff path by the waterfall. Along the river bank – running, running, running. Littlenose could hardly think. He had a stitch in his side, and he was gasping for breath. At last, he managed to cry: "What's the matter? Why are we running?" But Father only dragged him along faster.

At last, when Littlenose thought his legs would collapse under him, they reached the cave. Father pushed Littlenose inside. "Stay there!" he shouted, and dashed away again, shouting out to the people in nearby caves.

In a moment he was back, Mother by his side. She was carrying a large pot, and as she approached the fire, Littlenose thought: "Oh good! Dinner!"

But to his horror, she emptied the whole potful of water over the fire, which went out in a great steaming sizzle. Father began piling rocks in the entrance. Soon the cave was cold and dark, with only a few chinks showing through the barrier, and a black sooty puddle where the fire had been.

Two-Eyes had come inside just before rocks were piled in the entrance, and now, with Littlenose and Mother, he was bundled by Father into the back of the cave. Putting his fingers to his lips, Father tiptoed to the blocked-up doorway and peered through a hole. After a moment, he came back and said

in a low voice: "All clear, so far, but keep quiet. We don't want to take any chances."

Littlenose couldn't understand what was going on. "Mother," he whispered, "why are we hiding? Why did you put the fire out? Why did Father . . .?"

"The Straightnoses!" interrupted Father.

"What are the Straightnoses?" asked Littlenose.

"Monsters!" said Father. "They are more dangerous than the woolly rhinoceros, more cunning than the sabre-toothed tiger, and more destructive than a whole family of cave bears."

"What do they look like?" asked Littlenose. "They are horribly ugly," said Father, "and the worst part is that they look quite like us – at a distance. Close to they are hideous. Their heads are small and their necks long and thin. Their chins stick out, and their foreheads are high. And, worst of all, their noses are narrow and straight."

Littlenose looked at the large heads and short thick necks, the small chins and low foreheads of his beautiful Mother and handsome Father. He touched his own little round nose, and even *it* was better than an ugly straight one.

"They don't live respectably in caves like us," continued Father, "but roam the land together in great numbers, following the animal herds. They make their camps in the open. That was one of their camps we found this morning. They must have been somewhere in the neighbourhood, and we must lie low until they have moved on."

All through the chilly night, Littlenose and his parents huddled under furs and tried to sleep. Cold draughts blew in through the piles of rocks, and only Two-Eyes in his shaggy coat was warm and comfortable.

Next morning, Father pulled out one of the rocks from the doorway, squeezed through the hole, and slipped out of the cave. He was back

quite soon, calling to Mother and Littlenose to
come out. Two hunters had gone at dawn to
see if they could discover exactly where the
Straightnoses were. From a safe distance, they
had watched the whole tribe cross the valley,
and seen them disappear over the hills.

Caves were unblocked and fires were lit.
Everyone was very relieved that the danger
had passed, but Mother warned Littlenose that
he must be especially careful not to stray from
home. The tribe stayed close to their caves for

several days. But they had rather short memories, and the visit of the Straightnoses was soon forgotten.

Littlenose's memory was *particularly* short, and one day he and Two-Eyes set off to look for bees' nests. Littlenose was fond of honey, and he knew a very good place. As they left, a party of men was setting off to hunt, and they waved to Littlenose as they passed.

Littlenose didn't find any honey. All he found were a few broken scraps of honeycomb which had been left lying in the grass. He shared these with Two-Eyes.

There didn't seem to be much point in staying, so Littlenose and Two-Eyes set off for home. However, as it was still early, they went by a roundabout but much more interesting way. They had been walking for some time when they came on to the top of a low hill.

Below them, in the valley, a party of men was walking along in single file, carrying several dead animals slung from poles. "Look

Two-Eyes," said Littlenose, "it's the hunters going home. Let's join them and pretend that we are hunters too."

Shouting out to the hunters, he dashed down the slope with Two-Eyes at his heels. Two-Eyes was soon left far behind. The little mammoth just wasn't built for running in deep heather, and he quickly slowed to a walk.

The men had stopped when Littlenose first shouted, and now stood watching him. But they didn't call back or wave as Littlenose had expected. There seemed to be more of them than he had watched leaving the valley.

57

Then his Father's words came back to him: ". . . they look very like us – at least at a distance." Littlenose hesitated, but he was too late. Even as he realised that these men must be Straightnoses, they were after him. He ran as fast as he could, but he was already breathless, and in a moment they were on him. He was lifted, wriggling, into the air, while the Straightnoses had a good look at him. Then he was dumped on his feet, one of them gripped him firmly by the arm and they continued their march.

Littlenose fought, scratched and bit, but the man holding him took no notice. He dragged him along whether Littlenose was on his feet or not. It was quite useless to struggle. So after a while, Littlenose just trotted tearfully along, hoping for a chance to escape.

They arrived at the Straightnoses' camp at dusk. It was in a sheltered hollow with a big fire burning in the centre, and several smaller ones here and there. There were crowds of

Straightnoses, men, women, and children.
Some were eating round the fires, and others
were sitting under shelters made of animal
skins hung from tree branches.

When they saw Littlenose, they came
rushing towards him, and he found himself in
the centre of a ring of very unfriendly faces.
They screamed and shouted at him with
strange high-pitched voices and Littlenose
couldn't understand. Then one of them
prodded him with a stick, then another, and

another. It was too much. With a sudden grab, Littlenose seized one of the sticks and charged, shouting at the top of his voice. The crowd scattered in front of him, but in a moment he was gripped from behind by one of the hunters. Tucked under the man's arm, he was carried towards the large fire in the middle of the camp.

"Oh dear," thought Littlenose, "I think they're going to cook and eat me."

He was put down on his feet again, and the next moment the crowd had parted, and a very tall figure stood before him. He seemed to be the leader, and looked rather splendid. He had several long feathers stuck in his hair, and a necklace of tigers' claws round his neck. He also wore a long robe of white fur.

He looked at Littlenose, and said something in a strange language.

Littlenose didn't want to risk making him angry, so he smiled, nodded his head, and said, "Yes, sir."

60

It was awful! The leader's face went a deep red, then he started shouting and yelling to the crowd, and they too shouted even louder than before.

Frantically, Littlenose shook his head and shouted, "No, no sir. Please, I didn't mean it. Please sir no!" And shook his head even faster.

Meanwhile, Two-Eyes had been following Littlenose and the Straightnoses. With his little trunk snuffling the ground in front of him, he had followed their trail. As darkness fell he found himself looking down on the camp. There was a dreadful noise of shouting and the little mammoth was quite bewildered with the flickering light of the fires and all the Straightnoses running about. Then suddenly he spotted Littlenose in a clear space by the big fire.

Straight away Two-Eyes charged down the slope. In the dark, his black fur made him invisible, and the Straightnoses were making so

much noise that they didn't hear him. He
rushed right into the camp! He could no
longer see Littlenose, but he put his head down
and charged.

With a crash, he smashed through one of the
skin shelters, toppling it to the ground. It fell
across a fire, and burst into flames. The grass
and bushes caught alight, so did more
shelters. The Straightnoses couldn't see
Two-Eyes. But they saw shelters falling and
flames bursting out all over the place. They

fell over each other. They fell over Two-Eyes. They thought it was the end of the world, as Two-Eyes went blundering and crashing through the camp, looking for Littlenose.

Littlenose was as frightened as the Straightnoses. So frightened that he didn't even think of running away when the Straightnoses bolted and left him standing. Then a dark shape came out of the shadows. A red eye and a green eye caught the light from the flames. With a shout of joy, Littlenose leapt up on Two-Eyes' back, and urged him to a gallop.

They charged through the crowd, Two-Eyes trumpeting as loudly as he could, and Littlenose making wild whooping noises as loudly as *he* could. A few men chased after them, but soon gave up as Littlenose and Two-Eyes disappeared into the darkness on the hillside. At the top of the slope, Littlenose and Two-Eyes looked back. The Straightnoses were still running to and fro shouting to each other. They seemed to have completely forgotten Littlenose. The moon was rising, and Littlenose and Two-Eyes, with one last backward glance, set off for home where Mother, Father and a warm cave were waiting for them.

Dozy

One day Littlenose and Two-Eyes came home soaking wet. They had been playing by the river, which was starting to freeze, and Littlenose had been testing the ice to see how strong it was. It had held him quite well, but, unfortunately, Two-Eyes had wanted to join him. The weight of the young mammoth had been too much, and they had both fallen through into the water. Luckily it wasn't very deep.

Now they stood at the cave entrance, with water dripping in puddles round their feet, and icicles beginning to form on Two-Eyes' fur.

Mother was furious. "What a stupid child you are, Littlenose, playing in the water in weather like this!" she scolded, and she chased

him into the cave to get dry. "Put on your best furs," she called. "We have a visitor coming, a very important visitor. The Old Man is coming to supper, and you must be on your best behaviour."

Littlenose was excited. The Old Man was leader of all the folk in the valley, and it was a great honour when he chose to visit a family.

The Old Man arrived just before sunset, and Mother had an enormous meal ready. Only Father and the Old Man ate together by the fire. Mother served them, while Littlenose crouched with Two-Eyes in the corner at the back of the cave.

First of all there was fruit; wild pears and
crab apples, hips, haws and brambles. And
then they had small trout which had been
caught that morning. While they were eating
this, Mother was busying herself by the fire,
where huge chunks of rhinoceros meat were
sizzling. Soon it was cooked, and the Old Man
and Father were tucking into it heartily.
Littlenose had his share of the feast too, and so
did Two-Eyes.

When Father and the Old Man had finished their meal, they sat back and called Mother and Littlenose to join them.

"That's a fine, sturdy lad you have there," said the Old Man, and Father beamed proudly. "What do you call him?" he asked.

"Littlenose," said Father.

"Well, Littlenose," said the Old Man, "are you a good boy? Do you obey your parents? Do you help them all you can?"

Littlenose looked at the ground and shuffled his feet.

"He usually means well," said Mother, "but he's always getting into trouble. Why, only today. . . ."

But the Old Man interrupted: "Tell me about today, Littlenose. What have you been doing? I was a boy once, you know, and I like to hear what mischief the youngsters of today get up to."

So Littlenose told the Old Man about his game with Two-Eyes by the river.

The Old Man laughed. "I wish I could have seen you," he said. "It must have been very funny when the ice broke."

"It wasn't at all funny when the two of them came dripping water all over the floor," said Mother. "I don't know which is the more stupid, Littlenose or his mammoth."

"I had a mammoth when I was young," said the Old Man, "and he gave no end of trouble."

"Do you still have him?" asked Littlenose.

"I'm afraid not," replied the Old Man, "but sit down here by me, and I'll tell you all about him."

Littlenose settled down at the Old Man's feet to listen to the story.

"My mammoth," began the Old Man, "was called 'Dozy'. He was full-grown and very handsome, but he had one fault; he was too fond of thinking. That's why I called him Dozy. If he saw something interesting, he would sit down for hours on end just thinking about it.

He sat in the rain – and wondered why it came down instead of going up. He sat in the snow – and wondered why it was white, and not black. He would watch a falling leaf, and squat down beside it, and think what the chances were of its rising up in the air and growing back on to the tree.

"Our tribe lived in a small valley on the edge of a trail through the hills. Every autumn, huge herds of elk came through on their way south, and the hunters would kill as

many as possible. The animals were cut up and
stored in special caves, where the winter
frosts froze them solid, to keep them good for
eating during the long dark days ahead.

"But one autumn there seemed fewer elk
than the year before, and the next year there
were fewer still. At last, one year, there were so
few that the hunters were able to kill all of
them, and even then, the tribe was very
hungry for most of the winter.

"The Old Man of the tribe gathered the
people together and spoke to them: 'If we
remain here, we shall certainly die of hunger,
but our hunters say there is an empty valley
with plenty of animals only seven days' march
across the plain. If we start now, we can be

settled in new homes when the first snow comes."

"But some of the people didn't want to leave their old homes so soon. They wanted to wait and see what happened.

"So we waited, and waited, but no elk came, and in the late autumn, when the trees were already turning to gold and brown, the tribe began the trek to new lands. We straggled in a long line across the grassy plain, and every evening we made camp around enormous fires, before pushing on next morning.

"Dozy found all this very interesting, and in fact I had great difficulty in getting him to move at all! The sight of everyone leaving their caves and setting off into the unknown,

73

fascinated him so much that he thought and thought. He would squat on his haunches, head on one side, and he was always the last to leave, after much pushing and kicking from me. This happened every morning, and the tribe had often disappeared from sight before Dozy stood up, and plodded after them in his own dreamy fashion.

"Each evening, Dozy was the last to arrive, and sometimes he was so late that he had hardly time to lie down before the next day's journey was beginning. Then, with only one more day to go before we reached the new valley, we woke to find the sky heavy and grey. A few snowflakes began to fall, and by the time we started, a blizzard was raging.

"The tribe couldn't do anything but wrap up in every fur they owned, and carry on.

"Dozy had never seen a real blizzard before, and he was very interested. He had been doing some very deep thinking about a burnt patch on his fur, which he had got one night when he

lay too close to one of the fires. He was so busy trying to make up his mind whether to move or not, that he had caught alight. He had only moved because I tried to beat out the flames and this had disturbed him.

"He managed to trudge a mile or so through the driving snow, before he decided to sit down and have a nice long think. He really enjoyed thinking about snow. This time we couldn't wait, the snow was getting worse all the time.

"The whole tribe stopped to help move him. We pleaded. We threatened. We pushed. We pulled. We tugged at his trunk, his tusks and his tail. But Dozy just would not be budged, and finally we all moved on, calling out to him to follow. When evening came, the tribe camped in the shelter of a rocky hill, and that night it was so cold that the rocks split open with a loud crack, and birds dropped dead from the sky. When morning came, the snow stopped. But there was no sign of Dozy.

"I hurried back across the plain, and there he was, just as I had left him. He was sitting in the snow – frozen hard as a stone.

"There was nothing I could do, and I went on my way with the tribe, hoping that the ice might melt in the spring, and Dozy would follow me to my new home.

"But that," said the Old Man to Littlenose, "was the last we ever saw of him. I never managed to go back and look for him and for all I know, he is there yet."

There was a silence for a moment when the Old Man stopped. Then Littlenose said: "When I grow up, I shall cross the great plain and find Dozy for you."

"I'm sure you will," said the Old Man.

Late that night, when everyone was asleep, Littlenose lay awake thinking about Dozy. He pictured him all alone, sitting in the middle of the plain thinking and thinking. Could he be still there? Could he have thawed out and got lost trying to find his master? Or – had there never been a Dozy? Was it only a story made up by the Old Man? "No," Littlenose decided. "Such a wonderful tale just *had* to be true."

One day, when the snow had melted, Father came home with wonderful news. A party of men was going on a long hunting trip, and Littlenose was being allowed to go too!

Littlenose set off with his Father and the other men early next morning – and by the end of the day he was bored, bored, bored! They had found no animals at all.

Next morning, when it was just light, Father pointed to a rocky hill. "Let's climb up there, and see if we can see anything," he shouted, and they hurried towards it.

As they went, Littlenose began to remember the Old Man's story. The great plain where they were hunting . . . a rocky hill. . . . Surely, this must be the place! He gazed all around, but could see nothing.

At the top of the hill, Littlenose tried to recall the details of the story, and strained his eyes looking away into the morning mist.

He saw all sorts of faraway objects, but as he looked longer, he saw they were rocks or bushes. Then he spotted a grey shape in the mist a long, long way away. He stared and stared. But it didn't become a rock. Nor did it become a bush. Littlenose's heart began to thump. Could it be . . . ? Littlenose looked harder. The mist had closed in and there was nothing but the rolling plain below. So he never knew whether he had seen Dozy or not.

The Ice Age has long since passed away, and the Neanderthal folk and many of the animals they knew have gone. But not very long ago, some hunters found something very unusual – a mammoth, sitting on the ground, frozen solid as a stone. It looked just as though it were thinking very hard. They took it to the Leningrad museum in Russia, and it is still there. And in the Royal Scottish Museum in Edinburgh, you can see the skeleton of the Great Elk, standing with its great antlers raised

MAMMOTH

and towering above the other land creatures.

The only people now are ourselves –
the Straightnoses – and our world is warmer
and safer. Littlenose's world was cold and
dangerous, but he was a happy little boy,
and that is what matters most, after all.